DOUBLE
OR
NOTHING

FAIR

by Catherine Daly
illustrated by Tammie Lyon

Kane Press
New York

For my parents, Babs and George.
With lots of gratitude to Matthew Anderson for his
extremely helpful and detailed lesson. And also for the
really cool squirrel. And special thanks to Nate Kolbeck
and 3D Brooklyn for their time, assistance,
and generosity. —C.D.

For my new puppy, Artie Lyon, who really is Double
Trouble and my husband, Lee, who let me rescue yet
another doggie! —T.L.

Library of Congress Cataloging-in-Publication Data
Names: Daly-Weir, Catherine, author. | Lyon, Tammie, illustrator.
Title: Double or nothing / by Catherine Daly ; illustrated by Tammie Lyon.
Description: New York : Kane Press, 2018. | Series: Makers make it work | Summary:
When Mia wins a one-of-a-kind dolphin statue at the fair, her twin brother Mason
wants it for his collection.
Identifiers: LCCN 2017023205 (print) | LCCN 2017038318 (ebook) |
ISBN 9781575659909 (ebook) | ISBN 9781575659893 (pbk) | ISBN 9781635920147
(reinforced library binding)
Subjects: | CYAC: Twins—Fiction. | Brothers and sisters—Fiction. |
Sharing—Fiction. | Three-dimensional printing—Fiction.
Classification: LCC PZ7.D175 (ebook) | LCC PZ7.D175 Dou 2018 (print) | DDC
[E]—dc23
LC record available at https://lccn.loc.gov/2017023205

10 9 8 7 6 5 4 3 2 1

First published in the United States of America in 2018 by Kane Press, Inc.
Printed in China

Book Design: Michelle Martinez

Makers Make It Work is a trademark of Kane Press, Inc.

Visit us online at **www.kanepress.com**

Like us on Facebook
facebook.com/kanepress

Follow us on Twitter
@KanePress

Mason and Mia were twins. Mia was older. Two and a half minutes older, to be exact. She was also three quarters of an inch taller than her brother. To be exact.

Mason did not like either of those facts one bit.

The twins agreed on a lot of things.

Chocolate was better than vanilla.

Third grade was harder than second. Hamsters were better than gerbils.

And Halloween was better than Valentine's Day.

But the twins also disagreed about a lot of things.

Who was better at math.

Who could stand on their head the longest.

And who had the best dolphin collection.

Their parents called it "Twin Troubles."

"Mason's pancake is bigger than mine," Mia pointed out at breakfast.

Mason counted. "Mia has three more blueberries than I have."

"I give up!" Their mom picked up the newspaper and began to read.

"Look!" Mason pointed at the newspaper. "The Frogville Falls Fair starts today!"

"Hot diggity!" said their dad.

The twins laughed. Their dad was goofy, but the Frogville Falls Fair really was awesome. Like the ad said, it was fun for the whole family.

The family piled into the car. Mia and Mason didn't even draw an imaginary line down the middle of the backseat. They were *that* excited.

At the fair, Mia spotted her favorite ride. "Let's go on the giant swings!" she called.

Mason was right behind her.

Mia and Mason were too busy having fun to have any Twin Troubles at all.

"Oh look—carnival games!" shouted Mason.
Their parents exchanged nervous glances.
"Wouldn't you rather check out the 3D
printer exhibit?" their mom asked hopefully.

"No, I want to beat Mia in Balloon Blast!" said Mason. He pointed to one of the prizes—a gleaming blue dolphin. The twins *loved* dolphins. This one would be perfect for Mason's collection.

Their parents sighed. The bell rang and they were off!

The twins aimed water into the
clowns' mouths. The balloons got bigger
and bigger until . . . **POP!**

"I won!" cheered Mia. The man handed her the dolphin.

"No fair." Mason pulled out another dollar. "I'll win my own," he said.

"Sorry, buddy," said the man. "That was the last one. But you could win this cool stuffed earthworm."

Mason's mouth fell open. Who wanted a stuffed earthworm?

For the rest of the afternoon, nothing made Mason happy.

Not the state capitol building sculpted out of butter . . .

or the biggest turnip in the county.

Not even the deep-fried ice cream.

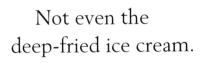

Mason tried to get over it, but all day Mia carried that dolphin everywhere. Or *almost* everywhere.

While she was taking her bath, he passed her bedroom door. The dolphin was on her dresser. Mason took it and placed it on his bookshelf next to his other dolphins. It looked like it belonged there.

It didn't take long for Mia to notice. "Mom! Dad! My dolphin is missing!" she cried. She ran into Mason's room. "You stole it!"

"I just borrowed it!" Mason shouted.

Their parents found them in a dolphin tug-of-war.

"Geez Louise," said Dad.

"That's it," said Mom. "Until you two can learn to share, I'm holding onto this dolphin."

The twins both scowled.

That night Mia dreamed her parents made her split the dolphin in two.

She woke with a start. The only way to get the dolphin back was to find the exact same one for Mason. But how?

In the morning, she called her grandmother and asked if they could go to the mall. They found dolphin T-shirts, necklaces, stuffed animals, and even underwear. But no perfect blue statues.

Mia went home and searched and searched online. Nothing.

The dolphin truly seemed to be one of a kind.

At school she told her best friend, Jen, the whole story as they walked down the main hallway. They passed by the office and saw someone using the copy machine.

"If only you could make a copy of your dolphin," said Jen with a laugh.

Mia sighed. "If only," she said.

That afternoon, her class took a trip to the town library. They learned the rules of the library, how to get a library card, and how to use the computers. Everyone left with a book.

On the way out, Mia saw something that made her stop in her tracks.

Suddenly she knew what she had to do!

3D PRINTER DEMONSTRATION TOMORROW 3:30 PM

The next day, Mia's mom dropped her off at the library. Mia made her way to the front of the crowd.

A young man stood by a medium-sized machine. "My name is Nate," he said. "And I'm here today to teach you about 3D printing. A 3D printer makes a solid object from digital files. We're going to make an exact copy of this mug before your very eyes."

Mia raised her hand. "Can we copy this instead?" She held up the statue.

Nate laughed. "I don't see why not," he said.

To print something with a 3D printer, you can make your own 3D design on a computer, find a 3D design on the internet, or scan an object.

Nate placed the dolphin on a turntable. He handed a small machine to Mia.

"We'll use this handheld 3D scanner to take pictures of the dolphin," Nate said. He slowly spun the dolphin so Mia could scan it from all sides.

Then Nate sent the scan to the computer. The image of the dolphin popped up onscreen. This was the 3D model they would send to the machine for 3D printing. They compared the dolphin onscreen with the one on the table.

"Its eyes look a little small," said Mia.

With a few clicks of the mouse, Nate made the eyes bigger.

"Perfect," said Mia.

Nate pointed to a spool attached to the printer. "The nozzle will spit out tiny strands of melted bioplastic, following the pattern we just made."

He showed Mia how to apply a thin layer of glue to the print bed. This would keep the 3D object in place as it was created.

"We're ready to start!" he told her. "Will you press this button, please?"

Mia did, and the printer began to work!

Bioplastic is a special kind of plastic that is made using sugar or corn instead of oil, like most plastic. It is compostable, which means it is good for the earth.

The nozzle went back and forth in strange patterns, laying down the melted plastic, layer by layer. It took a *very* long time. But finally it was done. Mia frowned. The dolphin looked weird and fuzzy. "Something went wrong!" she said.

Nate laughed. "That's just the support material," he told her. He handed Mia a putty knife. "Now you're on clean-up duty!"

Nate showed her how to pop the statue off the printer bed. Next he gave her a pair of pliers, sandpaper sticks, and goggles to protect her eyes.

> *Cleaning up* means removing the support material with pliers and sanding the object until it is smooth.

Mia worked hard to clean up the new dolphin. She worked even harder painting it when she got home. She wanted it to look perfect, and she wanted it to be ready by dinnertime.

At the dinner table, their parents looked
serious. "The dolphin is missing," their mom
said. "Who took it?"

"It wasn't me," said Mason.

Mia reached into her backpack and put the
dolphin on the table. "I'm sorry I took it without
asking," she said. "I had a good reason."

Then Mia pulled out the second dolphin. It looked exactly the same!

"Well, I'll be a monkey's uncle!" said their dad. "How in the world did you do that?"

"They had a 3D printer at the library!" said Mia. "We scanned the dolphin, printed it out, and I cleaned it up and painted it."

"That is so totally cool!" Mason smiled at his sister. "Now our dolphins are twins, too! Just like you and me."

"But don't forget, I came first," said Mia with a grin.

"You were just a warm-up," Mason shot back.

"Jiminy crickets," said their dad. "The Twin Troubles are back!"

Learn Like a Maker

3D is short for "three dimensional," which means that an object has height, width, and depth. When Mia used the 3D printer, it scanned all sides of her dolphin. Recording the object's height, width, and depth was important so that the printer could build an exact model of her dolphin.

Look Back

- ✖ Look back at page 22. Mia wanted Nate to scan her dolphin and create a 3D copy of it. What would you have asked Nate to scan?

- ✖ Reread pages 25–26. How is a 3D printer similar to a photocopier, which makes 2D copies? How is it different?

Try This!

3D Zoo
Suggested materials: paper, crayons, markers, recyclables, glue, tape, scissors, paint, fabric scraps, cotton balls, pipe cleaners, popsicle sticks

Fold a piece of paper into four rectangles. Draw a picture of your favorite animal from each side. These drawings are 2D because they don't have depth. Then use the materials you have available to create a 3D version of the animal in your picture. Once your sculpture is complete, compare it to the pictures you drew.